Upon The Generation of Life

Experimentation and Findings of the Indulgence of Animal
Electricity within the Stature of Man

Victor Frankenstein

University of Ingolstadt 1792

By KEV FREEMAN

A companion to

Frankenstein or the Modern Prometheus by Mary Shelley.

and

Frankenstein 2035 by Kev Freeman.

www.Frankenstein2035.com

for more information.

ISBN 978-1-7365709-7-5 (Paperback)

I begin this journal with anticipation this record of my endeavor will sometime provide others with a foundation for further experimentation into the independence of the human spirit.

Victor Frankenstein, October 1st, 1792

October 5th

Greater than two years have passed since I entered this university. Then my arms ached, loaded with the additional reading materials recommended by M. Waldman as I first stepped with trepidation towards the stairs to the lofty height of what would become my space. A dark, empty, and cold room which sat above all other accommodation.

Now the same space is my working laboratory, its volume filled with equipment gathered as a result of my studies and learning. My competency regarding the operation of these various machines and equipment grows day by day, and in some respects excels that of my tutors.

Along my walls bookshelves sit full of great works. Writings and episodes which reveal in their pages the secrets of the physical world. Some who read this document may still refer to such as nothing more than the fancied imagination of alchemic stupor.

The found works of Paracelsus, Albertus Magus, Nicolás Monardes, Sun Simiao, Dioscorides, Avicenna, Galen, Gaius Plinius, Masawaiyh, and Nicholas Flamel, which I continue to read with unrelenting vigor. They are more value than their weight, their texts pull back the shadowy veil which blinds us all.

For all this time destiny has continued to add to the many hours spent attending lectures and then also to my own studies. This morning, I climb the stairs to my laboratory with a newfound energy and nervous excitement. My steps no longer reluctant, my desire to test my theory against the supposed laws of the physical realm. It is today that I'm convinced I enter the final weeks of my discovery. The deepest mysteries of creation will soon open with a revelation to shake the foundation of human perception.

Progress, like scaling the most difficult mountainside is made with the knowledge failure will, without pause, propel many adventurers to the edge of the precipice, success will lead a few to the summit.

A culmination of sometimes coincidental events continues to encourage my effort. Only this last evening, I garnered welcome gains through the reading of a work, placed into my possession by invisible hands.

I suspect the book was deposited at my door by Waldman or one of his secretive acquaintances, the shadows who scurry around his quarters at late hours of the day. I hear mention of a secret society which follows Dean Weishaupt and infiltrates the university. There are murmurs of the King's displeasure at such interference.

Returning to the discussion of the book at hand, the document 'Cerebri Anatome', describes dissections of the human brain, performed by Dr Thomas Willis. I find excitement, especially in the areas of his theories of the cause of palsy and apoplexy. I consumed the pages a with great vigor, digesting the whole within the past evening.

I awoke this morning taken by a great fervor. The night filled with vivid dreams and visions, which sparked and flailed against the darkness like multi-colored fireworks. An intensity of excitement is stoked like a newborn fire by the most remarkable and unusual actions of Dr Willis, in particular his renown relating to resuscitation of the dead.

In evidence, I find a case in which he brought to consciousness the lifeless body of a young woman many hours after her public hanging and pronouncement of death.

The recordation of the execution and subsequent recovery notated in the writing's contained within an accompanying publication, which I also have in my hands, from the same source I may add, entitled: 'Newes from the dead or a true and exact narration of the miraculous deliverance of Anne Greene.'

Upon deposit of the lifeless body of the girl to a place of its proposed dissection, Dr Willis, convinced the spirit remained within, subsequently applied many techniques in attempt to reattach the will to its bodily form. After long effort, encompassing many hours, the young woman subject of his effort sprang back to life. More remarkably, she regained her full vigor some two weeks after her supposed death.

The result of his interaction led Dr Willis, towards a conviction that 'Animal Spirits', are generated in the brain and can be summoned to rejoin the body. Willis also affirms these 'Animal Spirits' are only propagated in the brain and cerebral core. From this double fountain they cascade out into all the rest of the parts, and illuminate, by a constant influence, the whole nervous system. It was most opportune that this document came into my possession as it supports my own theory and provides sustenance to this work.

Willis also proposes a signal is thence driven and diffused through the nerves like rays of light to thereby facilitate animal life through nervous re-action. Obstruction of these 'Animal Sprits' would therefore lead to symptoms of palsy and weakness.

I find with equal relevance and importance to my work that Dr Willis demonstrated the interconnectivity of the capillaries and veins of the brain through his experimentation. Of this I need to examine in detail.

His discovery of the communication between the canals of vessels which connect to water the whole head, is of essence to the delivery of a life-giving substance, yet to be found, which may therefore facilitate the return of the spirit.

October 6th

A greater germination of thought and study surrounds the reasoning of one Luigi Galvani and many others in the potential use of the discovery of 'Animal Electricity' as a vital component in the viability of life.

Prior to my arrival, I became knowledgeable of the extensive experimentation of Galvani. His discoveries around 'Animal Electricity' and its engagement to cause contractions to frog muscle by the simple placement of wires of different metals, namely, an iron wire to the muscle and a copper wire to the nerve.

Today I intend to engage such experimentation upon various limbs and muscles in the hope of being able to replicate the results. However, instead of the frog, or other animal such as the cat or dog, upon which Galvani's and other's research have been focused, I will study the human form. The foundation of alchemy will be employed. I am convinced through the most appropriate combination between Galvanism and the intention of 'Animal Electricity' will be discovered.

The awareness of the fact an animal body can be directed to make convulsive movements when electricity is not directly applied to the nerve is of prime relevance. The metallic arc being the essential moment and the essence of the attraction of the spirit, which surely drives the connection.

I note that others, in replicating Galvani's earlier experiments, found that two different metals, silver, and zinc, were the most efficient combination to elicit reaction in the subject. These metals, when laid in contact with the circuit to be animated, could communicate with the part to be excited.

However, there are instances observed, which seem to have proved an alternative. Dr Baillie of London also discussed Galvani's discovery and committed that he had twice or more produced contractions of frog legs by the application of a singular metal only.

As this method would carry a greater efficiency about it, I will undertake my own experiments which I will detail further.

For the whole time of my study, I have acquainted myself thoroughly in the anatomy of the human form and observed in great detail the natural decay and corruption of the human body. After death. This knowledge will now be applied solely to the generation of life within a human vessel.

All of my work will depend upon the procurement of cadavers in better state of preservation than those which I have received previously, each in the later stage of postmortem.

The energies and virtues of man can be broken down into

the *Sensitive* and to the *Motive*:

The *Sensitive* is those interactions and receptors of the external functions of touching, smelling, tasting, hearing, and seeing.

The *Motive*, being in my thought the definition of the human spirit. Those evidenced by the possession of an imagination to take into the mind a thing for investigation and the possession of a memory which can be accessed to remember the thought.

The direction of my work is therefore set. My aims are such:

Firstly, to fathom an elixir, which in its purpose is to re-energize the dormant cells of the brain and nervous system so that the Motive can be invited.

Secondly, to capture and infuse the animal spirit into a revitalized human vessel in order to provide a foundation for operation of the Sensitive.

My equipment and materials are set in place. I will commence my experimentation within the next week, upon delivery of suitable human cadaver, which I find are plentiful if recovered quickly from their place of burial if no care is given as to how they arrived at such a point.

October 8th

I have delivery of a body. A man some sixty years of age. The failure of the heart and other organs leading to a natural death. Damage and wear is such that parts suitable for experimentation are therefore limited to the limbs alone.

The beginning is now set. I have intent to find whether the use of one metal only will engage the 'animal electricity' as Dr Baillie purports. To this end I set equal proportions of Silver, Zinc, Brass, Copper, and Zinc as probes.

Experiment I

The subject limb is prepared. The left leg amputated below the hip, where the femur attaches, and the sciatic nerve exposed. A probe prepared from each of the metals to be

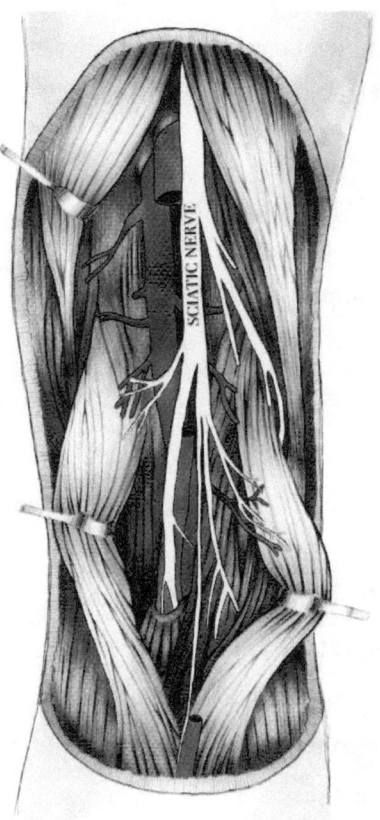

tested, which will be applied in turn upon the sciatic nerve of the dissected left leg of the man. The limb lying in a sufficient depth of clean water to allow some inches below the surface, the nerve projecting above and laid against a section of lint.

For each of the metals I make observations. Each probe is set out against the sciatic nerve independently. I am insulated from the table by a wooden stool. The results are recorded such:

Silver – No reaction

Copper – No reaction

Zinc – No reaction

Brass – No reaction

Iron – No reaction

After ten contacts, with the probes attached gently then with pressure against the exposed nerve, I failed to register any response and therefore could not replicate the results of Dr Baillie by application of one metal only. I reconfigured the experiment to use two metals.

Experiment II

I contacted the part of the nerve laying above the surface with a piece of a metal. But when the metal touched it at the surface, so that both the metals were in contact with the water, although the zinc was at the same time many inches removed from the limb, contractions were produced equally vigorous, as if both the metals had been in immediate contact with the skin.

The metals were then applied in turn using zinc as the partner, being placed within the water.

Silver – A strong reaction which increased with the number of applications.

Copper – Not as virile as the silver but with a similar proportional increase as the applications progressed

Zinc – Medium contractions, sustained.

Brass – Small contractions

Iron – The convulsions returned but with lower intensity.

The pairings demonstrated that the strongest contractions were obtained with a pairing of silver and zinc.

I therefore return to the use of silver and zinc as the partners with the knowledge a liquid conductor would be the most appropriate to connect the energy through to the nerves and muscles of the subject to be revived as a whole.

October 10th

Having established the most efficient combination of the two metals used for the generation of 'Animal Electricity', a base contact of zinc will be paired with a silver probe. The Nairne electrical machine will be used to deliver a constant electrical fluid. The purpose is to establish the most appropriate carrier of the recipe for life into the human body.

Experiment III

The liquids to be tested must neither be too hot nor too cold in the degree. The liquid must be well balanced with the blood and keep it in good fortune. The following liquids will therefore be tested:

i.   Spring Water,
ii. Water which has been distilled by boiling,
iii. The juice of the lemon,
iv. The milk of a cow its fat being skimmed,
v.   Water taken from the sea being extremely salty to the taste.

A sample of live blood taken from my own arm is laid equally within five jars. A half amount by volume of each of the fluid to be tested is added to the jars. Upon mixing the reactions are noted and the jars left for a period of one hour then observed again.

The passing of the hour revealed a distemper between the solutions containing the milk and the juice of a lemon. These were therefore removed from further testing.

Experiment IV

I removed from the same donor hand a finger, placing one each in the solutions to be tested. The electric machine was connected to the fingernail of each. A silver probe being inserted between the underside of the nail and the tissue beneath.

A plate of zinc was laid to be submerged within the combined solution and a steady electric fluid applied. The results of each connection are considered against one another such:

i.   Spring Water / Blood – The finger contracted steadily with a medium contraction.

ii.   Distillated Water / Blood – Contractions of the lowest degree.

iii.   Sea Water / Blood – Powerful contractions which remained steady.

In conclusion the mixture containing sea water demonstrated itself as being the greatest conductor of Galvanic force. It is therefore with this in mind I continue my discovery.

October 15th

After waiting with little patience for days for a subject, I have on this day the use of a complete body of a man recovered only last evening. My nerves are at their most delicate, having slept little between.

I carefully separate the head, ensuring the spinal cord is severed cleanly with minimum damage to the bone, nerves and tissues which protect it. The whole head then set apart, wrapped in cotton muslin and placed in a jar of cold water, being fully immersed.

Experiment V

The body, with head removed, was laid upon a plate of zinc. I stood upon an insulated chair, which communicated with the prime conductor connected to the electrical machine.

The machine put into action, and both I and the body were electrified positively. In these circumstances, no energy could be drawn from the body, by myself, nor could any other electrical appearance take place between us.

But, when a piece of silver was passed over different parts of the body, and, at the same time, brought into contact with the zinc plate, contractions were uniformly excited, differing not in the least, either in strength or frequency, from those which are excited when no artificial electricity is present. The result was precisely the same when the body and I were negatively electrified.

October 16th

<u>*Experiment VI*</u>

The following experiment was made, in order to observe whether the effect produced upon the body, by the passage of artificial electricity from any part of its form, would be increased by employing two different metals as conductors.

Again, the body was laid, successively, upon a number of different metals, iron, copper, tin, and steel and insulated upon glass. The body of the man was thereafter positively electrified by communicating with the prime conductor of an electrical machine. The contractions produced in the body, thus disposed, by drawing sparks from it, with metals different from those on which it was placed, were not stronger, than those occasioned by drawing similar sparks from it, with conductors of the same metal.

In establishing a communication between two opposite electricity's, as, for example, between the two sides of a charged phial, it is matter of indifference to which the conductor is first applied.

But it is by no means so, in the case of muscles and armed nerves. For, if one branch of a conductor be applied to the metal arming a nerve, before the other branch has been applied to the muscles, it frequently fails to excite contractions. However, if first applied to the muscles, this is very seldom the case.

October 17th

Experiment VII

Last evening, I received a complete cadaver of a young man, previously in good health and vitality. The cause of death was by execution through hanging some two days before delivery to my laboratory.

I preceded to amputate the right leg, having applied a tight ligature, as near as possible to the joint with the hip. The body had lain fully two days without circulation of blood, at the same time had been preserved by an unseasonably low temperature, resulting in a thick ground frost for the days which the body had lain in the ground.

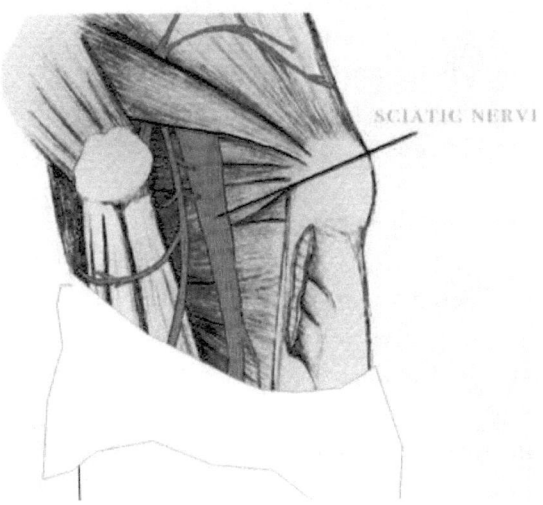

SCIATIC NERVE

The sciatic nerve was separated and exposed. The limb was laid upon zinc, and excited with silver it reacted most violently and convulsed for more than an hour. I continued to measure the convulsions for more than ten hours, they continued during several hours afterwards.

5 p.m. – immediate convulsions.

6 p.m. – still strong convulsions.

7 p.m. – powerful convulsions, easily gained.

8 p.m. – no change in convulsion and power.

9 p.m. – slight decrease in power.

10 p.m. – frequency of convulsions less.

11 p.m. – frequency diminished by one forth.

12 p.m. – steady convulsions.

1 a.m. – some diminishment of power.

2 a.m. – half initial convulsion rate.

3 a.m. – weakened convulsions, less regular.

Thereafter sporadic convulsions and twitching.

October 18th

Experiment VIII

I return to my notes being most encouraged. Taking the amputated left leg and hip of the recently executed man, I undertook a sectioning of the gluteus maximus and exposed the sciatic nerve. The limb then bathed in a solution of clean cold spring water, placing upon the muscle an extracted nerve, which for some time has detached from surrounding parts.

The nerve itself carefully positioned to remain laid upon a

lint free cloth until the moisture of the nerve has evaporated. It can excite no contractions in the muscles, to which, distributing by touching it alone with any two metals in contact with each other.

But, if the dry nerve receives moisture with a few drops of the solution, contractions instantly take place if I place the nerve in contact with zinc. Thus, I can realize convulsions through use of the conducting spring water with the silver rod attached to the toe of the foot.

October 19th

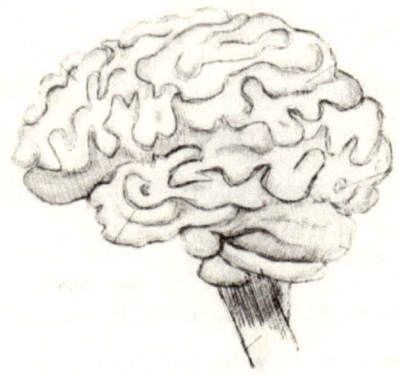

The human brain, a gelatinous organ which holds in its form the spirit within its cortex. Many fibrous pathways in turn connect the spirit to the body. The one certain product of the disconnection of these pathways is death, but this should not be the end of the enigma that is life, can I find a way to return the spirit to its natural place?

It must be that the answer to the largest of all questions is promulgated by determining how this structure, in all its magnificence, can be positioned to re-ignite. And then from a natural process of Galvanic 'Animal Electricity' to announce life. Maybe not the whole of life it previously knew, but a new life with its own memories and desires.

Experiment IX

The head, decapitated from the body utilized in experiment II, now more than four days since death, but held at temperatures close to zero Celsius will be the subject of this experiment.

Three zinc roundels, each the size and thickness of a silver 1 Thaler coin, were placed within the mouth and below tongue. The head was immersed whole, on its side, in a solution of clean water. I observed no reaction of any of the facial tissues., I placed the silver rod at the base of the neck, and at various parts upon the lesion. I observed a quite dramatic effect. As the rod was positioned and motioned around the stub, various facial muscles twitched and convulsed.

At one point, when the silver was in contact with the spinal cord, the left eye opened and stared directly at me. It was clear, though, as the pupil remained dilated when the light of a candle was drawn close that no independent control is being formed by this experiment.

It is my conclusion that the fabric of the brain itself, and therefore of the mind it contained, had already deteriorated beyond redemption prior to the

induction of galvanic force and its animal electricity. Further, it is also my conjecture that unless the underlying fabric supporting the action of the brain is restored, further progress will be negligible.

October 20th

Galvanism is successful only in the electrification of muscle movement. It does not offer the solution to the creation of independent thought. If I can only connect the two, then there is some chance that the mechanics of man will unwind to be welded together again to engage the ether of the spirit. Like parts of a clockwork, gears locking together to create a viable working mechanism. For it is only then independent movement and control will forcefully coerce the vessel to become an enabler of life.

Therefore, the vigor of brain and nerve cells must be restored to encourage the reattachment of the spirit to the vacant vessel. Moreover, the vessel needs to be in such a viable and engaging state so as to provide a suitable receptacle for the spirit to sustain a hold.

To promote such activity, I must experiment upon substances which are said to be essential to life itself and even provide longevity if applied in the correct proportions. I have at my hand a copy of the 'Pharmacopoeia Londinensis', from which I shall take direction.

The Compounds, selected upon varied dependence on one or more of specific property. Whereby, each would have affinity for acid, alkaline, salty, acrid, aromatic, spirituous, viscous, glutinous, oily, or aqueous conditions.

i.   Urine of a boar.
ii.   Juice of the cucumber.
iii.   Powder of the Japanese star anise.
iv.   Albumen of a hen's egg.
v.   Opium.
vi.   Arsenic.
vii. Liquoris.

viii.   Guano of the pigeon.

ix.   Juice of asparagus.

x.   A reduction of glycine and ethanol.

xi.   Juice of a Grapefruit.

xii.   Crushed bark of a willow tree.

October 21st

The reconstruction of the tissues of the brain is now my greatest focus and fear. For the brain will hold the spirit and it must be in condition to support the most positive emotions possessed by the most respected of our species. Mirth, joy, hope, humility, integrity, courage, creativity are my wants. Conversely the base depressive conditions of sadness, sorrow, stubbornness, jealousy, hatred, and revenge must be displaced and left with no room to thrive.

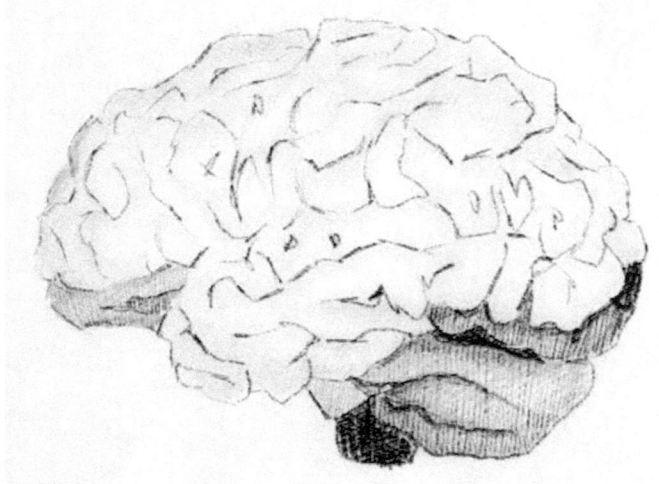

Experiment X

The brain of the subject cadaver is dissected. A number of
vials set with equal slices of brain matter, each submerged
in an equal quantity of one eighth part of a litron of
distillated water.

The compounds are introduced individually to the vials,
and gently circulated so as to be in contact with the matter
of the brain. Thence a galvanic influence provided equally
to each through a zinc base and silver rod applied directly
to the tissue. The vials then left for a period of twelve
hours.

October 22nd

The results of the previous days experiment have about them a revelation.

The following vials issued a response, which although positive, was not substantial enough to detect a resounding improvement in the tissues, i, iii, iv, viii, ix, and x. As for the others, the material in the vial had decayed and most rancid gases were produced.

Experiment XI

I therefore set about forming various solutions having carefully measured ratios of combinations of the six successful compounds.

The next days will be spent marking the results of as many combinations as possible, for there must be a success amongst one of them.

Combinations

A: i, iii, x.

B. i, iii, ix.

C. iii, iv, x.

D. iv, viii, ix.

E. viii, ix, x.

F. i, ix, x.

G. viii, iv, ix.

H. i, iv, viii.

October 23rd

I observe some progress with mixtures of all compounds when applied to the tissue of the brain.

Combination A – Positive, most improvement yet seen, but central areas of the tissue remained dull, as though a barrier to communication with the nutrients had been drawn upon the tissue.

Combination D - Most encouraging growth and reaction to galvanic interaction. For the most part, the tissue was easily separated, cohesion of the cells remains poor.

However, the organization of the tissue in all samples remains too weak, and I theorize that a binding agent will be required to facilitate regrowth. More investigation will be required to establish a substance which will aid in the process. The experiment continues overnight.

October 24th

On this day a great accident occurred overnight. Or should I say the greatest coincidence? Fungi growing upon rotten timbers within the roof area above the table on which the vials were set, fell into three of the open containers being studied. Having first been in a despondent mood I took to disposing of the vials and their contamination in a rage of disappointment.

Before I did so, and on closer examination my mood becomes lighter and then one of extreme joy, even one of rapture. The fungi, instead of causing a decay in the samples into which they had fallen had generated themselves within. The filamentous threads of the mold expanded and attached to the brain matter and caused a strengthening of the tissue in each sample. This event, a pure chance, revealed the mycelial threads of these mushrooms could act to bind flesh and tissue. The filaments when in contact with the solutions provided a foundational structure. Their function doubling the influence of the compounds as the threads also acted as a conduit for nutrients and water.

The final combination, which some will say should have been the first, uniting all the positive compounds, exhibited the most responsive result, which when the mycelial threads where added, increased its efficacy tenfold or greater.

Excitingly I had formed the essential pathway towards the base of life.

October 25th

My previous findings caused the introduction of filtered sea water to replace the distilled water as a carrier of the components.

As now known, it is most remarkable in that the solution has a multiple purpose - it acts as a conductor! The liquid provides a connection with the energy, converting it to a powerful amount of 'animal electricity'.

Today a great tiredness hit me. I shall resume when my energies return.

October 28th

I have slept for several days in an uneasy restless state of many visions and dreams. One such dream relayed a message - If I am to sustain life in a human form for any time worthy of consideration of success, then I must find a method for maintaining a supply of the blood for such life.

Then this is my next challenge. The issues are twofold.

The first relates to ensuring the blood is in circulation prior to the instigation of the process of establishing a flow of animal electricity. The second relates to the condition and viability of the blood to carry the spirit through the body.

In terms of the viability of the blood I have considered a number of recipes and potions as listed in the 'Pharmacopoeia Londinensis', in particular those concerning the vitality of the heart, liver, and the vital spirits which they maintain. The blood which I let from the bodies which I receive becomes thick with putrefaction soon after circulation ceases. It is therefore of great importance the process is halted and all filth is removed from the blood. The resultant solution will be required to comfort the heart and vital spirits, strengthen the activity of the brain, heart, and all internal organs.

Experiment *XII*

A sample of blood not exceeding one half litron is drawn from a rabbit after drowning in cold water and placed into a jar cooled by surrounding with cold water. The blood is left to stand in the jar for one hour, during which time it is observed to thicken slightly. The following mixture of compounds is ground together and placed within clean cotton lint and tied as a filter ball through which the original blood shall pass.

Celondine: The greater root of which is manifestly hot and dry, cleansing scouring the actions of the liver.

Succory: Cools and dries in the second degree, strengthens the liver and veins, opens obstructions in the liver and spleen.

Consolida major: A cold quality according to Dioscorides, will join wounds and heal ruptures.

Termerick: Hot in the third degree, opens obstructions.

Doronicum: Avicenna the Persian describes the hot and dry root acting to strengthen the heart.

Orris, or flower-de-luce: Hot and dry in the third degree, help in the breathing.

Stinking Gladon: Hot and dry in third degree, softens swellings, settle bruises, and aid the lungs.

Pimpernel: Something both hot and dry and are of such a drawing quality which Galen advises to help impurities of the liver.

Dictamny: A remedy against wounds, from the tale told by Virgil in the Aeneid.

Purslane: Cold and moist in the second degree, to act against inward inflammation as it cools the blood and liver.

Saffron: Powerfully concocts and rids the blood of toxin, driving back inflammation.

Senna: Heats in the second degree and dries in the first. Masawaiyh purports the substance helps the heart, liver, spleen and preserves youth.

Rosemary Flowers: Hot and dry in the second degree. Strengthen the brain and memory.

Citron Seed and the outward peel of the fruit – Strengthen the heart and liver and reduce the thickness of the blood.

Cauliflower Seed: Cleaning agent and to reduce heat by factor of two.

Sorrel: Moderately Cold and dry, cools the brain and blood.

Agrimonia: Hot and dry in the first degree, according to

Pliny, helps inward wounds, impurities of the liver, spleen and helps the jaundice.

The filter is placed between the jar containing the blood and an empty container of equal volume tied on to its top. The components are inverted, and the blood is filtered by gravity into the empty receptacle. The impurities are removed, and the blood thereby conditioned ready for use.

A living rabbit, in perfect health and vitality is connected to the reconditioned blood while its femoral artery is drawn until the filtered blood fully engorges the animal.

Other than some resistive discomfort the rabbit maintains attached to life for the remainder of the day.

With this success I will move towards experimentation upon a human cadaver when I receive one of adequate quality.

October 29th

Today I seek the methodology of establishing and sustaining the flow of blood through the body to enable the spirit to maintain the process independent of intervention.

Experiment XIII

I prepared a body of a man in older age which I received yesterday evening. The cause of death in the subject was related to a weakness of the heart. I attempted, with

Galvanic intervention, to create contractions which due to the damage did not respond.

I then resorted to the use of a heart of a pig, procured from the local slaughterhouse. The shape and form of the animal heart comprehends closely with that of the human. I tested the heart for its voracity between the zinc and silver plates. The convulsions were strong. Upon removal of the damaged heart, I connected the major arteries and veins of the pig heart to the human counterparts and placed within the cavity of the chest.

Connections were made at the femoral circulatory region of the man's leg to the blood cleaning jar. The pig heart was then caused to convulse, and the circulatory system activated. After a period of 1 hour all the blood from the body had been passed into the filtered jar and back into the system. This would be the process that I shall use to deliver a reservoir of clean blood to use in the final experiment.

Experiment XIV

I set out the foot of the body used in the previous experiment and observed the current of blood flowing slowly within the veins and capillaries. The rate in my mind would not be sufficient to guarantee the success required of the circulatory system to support a reanimation process.

A thin plate of zinc was introduced between the fleshy part of the foot at the base of the heal, and a silver probe used as an excitor and attached to the toe. I observed the circulation which appeared to be remarkably quickened several times when the metals were maintained in contact.

In conclusion, the addition of galvanic energy to the areas of low circulation does seem to aid the strength of the circulation of blood at the extremities of the body.

I therefore intend to attach a series of additional galvanic intersections at points of the body which would support the mechanical action of the heart. Which in turn of the implanted pig heart would be the original organ stimulated in its natural place.

November 3rd

After monitoring the samples, I arrive at a point of jubilation. Hence my remarkable discovery, my recipe, not found by any other who has sought the solution to this elusive mystery. My divine illumination being nothing greater than my findings. Findings arriving from many combinations of organic substances which I have discovered influence the construction and health of brain neurons and their function. From these experiments I hereby notate the secret.

The following measures of the required compounds, which when reduced from solution, combine within a liquid transport of filtered sea water to enable the restoration of function of the human brain.

Adding each measure to a volume by weight of half of a litron, I administered the proper volume to the brain. The interaction it produces energizes a spark of life, accelerated by the electricity carried within the nervous system itself. The compounds within this recipe are noted such.

The recipe as formulated

Pig Urine oxidized by electromagnetic energy. (2 parts)

The powder of the Japanese star anise, Illicium anisatum. (1 part)

The white of one chicken egg. (4 parts)

Bird guano dissolved within an equal volume of distilled water. (3 parts)

Filamentous fungi as found as the mycelial threads of mushrooms. (1 part)

Hydrolysis of asparagine, the compound being isolated from the juice of asparagus, by application of lead hydroxide. (2 part)

A reduction of glycine and ethanol. (2 part)

This fluid, consolidated as a growing compound, the essential mixture, or elixir, as I have named it, will only manifest its treasure when directly contacting the recipient tissues.

The body's own mechanical system must be used to transport the fluid. Feeding the vital fluid without obstruction into the cavity between the cranium and brain ensures maximum exposure and absorption. The contact establishing, over a period of no less than twenty-four hours, a structural foundation to the previously dead, inert brain.

As the organ becomes imbued with the solution, it opens itself to the influence of 'animal electricity'. Evident in the resultant motion of the nervous system and muscles of the subject. Thereafter, an excitement of contractions of the body will begin. Twitching, responding in its own time and without order.

November 4th

It then requires thought as to the establishment of a consistent method, a requirement for introducing this life fluid to the brain. This is certainly the only viable way of realizing the benefits of the mixture. It can only properly display the results through intimate contact with the cells which need repair. The priority is not the generation of new connections between, but the reconnection and reinforcement of existing patterns. In this way, the rediscovery of memories may be achievable. They store them themselves in a place which is yet to be discovered.

My efforts thereafter turned to the possibility of a direct infusion of the substances to the tissue itself. I consider and relate the options. The most importance of the alternatives is to achieve the most direct route possible. The method must be one which is limiting the invasive procedures as far as possible.

November 5th

Preparation of the head and brain.

Experiment XV

Drilling a small hole within the skull cap, ensuring that no damage caused to the underlying tissue of the brain, provided the opening. Access to the meninges being established, I worked carefully to carve my way through the dura.

This procedure was the most difficult as we find the layer

to have a toughness, which requires delicate effort to pierce. Working my way through to the arachnoid, resulting in some discharge of fluid, revealing the pia mater. Then, with the smallest and most discrete effort, the outer protective membranes of the organ pierced.

With a suitable sized rubber tubing attached to the opening of the skull, I connected the vial of life fluid, hoping gravity would do the work. However, the fluid system of the brain and spinal systems, being no long in an active state, did not provide volume to accommodate the additional liquid.

My remedy to this issue was a simple one, one that is of the most common sense. I introduced a spinal tap to the lower region of the spinal cord where it had been severed. In this method, the redundant volume, approximately one tenth of a litron of cerebrospinal fluid, flushed from the system to be replaced by the revitalizing compounds

I added the solution until it filled the cavity to overflow. I returned the output from the spinal tap to the vial, a closed loop system being formed. Thereafter, the life fluid circulated throughout the brain and the circuitous nervous system.

A connection to a previously a stored supply of Lavoisier's dephlogisticated air, the invisible substance he recently extracted from the wind around all of us. The product which imbues energy to flame and to life by greater than six times the normal. I manufactured a great quantity by heating the red calx of mercury with a burning glass.

I set the head as I had done before, within solution of seawater (having been filtered through many layers of cotton weave), repositioning two zinc roundels within the mouth. And set the galvanic rod to one side.

The gas was brought to the jar containing the head and thereafter sealed.

The whole will now be left upright for a single day to allow the building and reconstruction of the fibers of the brain. I enjoyed the wildest hope of an establishment of a viable connection between them. For the first time in months of experiment, I tasted the success upon my tongue.

November 6th

I awoke after a night of turmoil, my mind weighed with expectation. No need for breakfast today, no time to wait, for the result of the previous days experiment would deem my life work a success, or one of stumbling failure.

As I climbed the stairs to the laboratory the hairs on the back of my neck raised as I visioned the jagged edges of the misaligned and decayed teeth clamping down upon my fingers, although the action would be some sort of macabre sign of success, I humored to myself.

At the end of the second day, I removed the head from the jar and set it within its place. I moved to running the silver rod against the neck and spinal column. For a moment, no reaction followed. Then at once, with a sudden movement enough for me to lose grip of the rod, the face gained features it has not had since life departed at its last breath.

With sudden action, both eyes opened wide and flittered around with a half-purpose. As though hunting for a subject to focus upon.

The eyelids and lips worked in irregularly rhythmic contractions for about four seconds until the spasmodic movements ceased. The muscles within the face relaxed, the eyelids half closed, leaving only the pale yellow of the conjunctiva visible.

I operated the probe vigorously against the stem of the spinal cord. The action caused the eyelids to slowly lift up with an even movement, quite distinct and normal, such as happens in everyday life, with people awakened or torn from a dream.

The eyes and their pupils focused themselves, then with a defined purpose fixed their gaze upon my face. It was clear that I was not dealing with a vagueness without any expression.

I was dealing with undeniably intelligent action, eyes that lived, eyes which were looking at me. After several seconds, the eyelids closed again, slowly, with tiredness, and the head took on the same appearance as it had before I had applied the probe.

I repositioned the probe, varying its point of contact and, once more, without any spasm, slowly, the eyelids opened, and the eyes gradually fixed themselves with perhaps even more determination than the first time.

After their close there was no further movement, the eyes taking on the glazed look which they have in the dead.

My senses could not comprehend the magnitude of the event. The brain was active but did not engage a stable or lasting consciousness, the brain matter had begun to reconnect and welcome back the departed spirit. The experiment has worked.

My mind recounted the experiments of Antoine Wiertz and his accounts of life after decapitation and hoped that I had not caused such descriptions of suffering as he supposed. But instead had returned the spirit, pulling it through the bright window which is the entrance to heaven.

The compounds of life distilled. I have found the recipe which engages the spirit, once released to the ether, to return to inert flesh without resistance. The bridge between death and life connecting the elements. Compounds mixed with a solution and then circulated to be in contact with the biological fabric of human tissue will revitalize its energy.

I know now, the fluid, a precise reconstruction with a certain ratio, manifests a mechanism where energy becomes unrestricted, imbuing expired matter to live again.

November 8th

Today I received a severely mutilated body of a male who met his end due to a violent accident. The body was well preserved but itself has severely injured limbs and internal organs. So much to a tortuous extent.

Driven by my excitement at its height, I endeavor to repair the damage caused to the body rather than await a delivery of a specimen which may be in better condition.

Over the next days and nights, I shall prepare and assemble the necessary parts of the subjects' anatomy from my previous dissections and new remains secured in recent days from the place of their burial. It is, through grafting and reconnection, my aim to construct the most remarkable, astounding vessel to carry a revived spirit, a new man.

The work to prepare a frame for the reception of the spirit will be a task of immense complication. The binding of many different parts, muscles, veins will challenge every skill developed during the last two years.

I carry the weight of doubt of whether I should attempt the creation of such a complex form to carry the spirit. But my success has proven my ability. I have the base materials at hand to start this arduous an undertaking. Whether I succeed will depend upon my ability to work through the difficulties which will test me over the next days and nights. I fear my nervousness will not allow rest until the vessel is together.

November 27th

The past sixteen days has involved me in the construction and assembly of a new being, a new man ready to receive a reborn spirit.

I have attached legs and arms, extending the framework of each to the maximum possible. The head taken from a practically undamaged body of a man in his mid-twenties. The only replacement was that of the eyes, of which the complexity of connection took more than two days to achieve.

The abdomen of a man previously employed as a farm laborer, until his demise under a steam locomotive a week ago, is used as the base. The muscular development and general fitness will be a substantial base for my creation.

Internal organs such as, heart, lungs, liver and kidneys are replaced with younger aged organs.

Preparation of the clean blood taken from three separate donor cadavers recovered only yesterday is ongoing and will soon be complete.

The frame is complete and laid within a bath of salted ocean water.

November 28th

There are many parts of the complicated structure of any creature that caries life with it. I asked myself many questions, but the one vital answer I sought was whence did the principle of life proceed? For many weeks and months, my experiments and dissections sought a singular clue to the spark for which I sought the light. I understood death, the fundamental entropy that ended life. To determine that life was more than a supernatural side product. The many examples I exhumed from the ground in various states of decay led to the discovery of a most astonishing a secret. I revealed the cause of generation and life. From which I hold the capability of implanting spiritual host within previously lifeless matter.

Today is the full moon phase and therefore brings with it the maximum effect upon the brain and the connections it will seek to make of its own accord. The astronomical effect amplified by the position of the planet Mercury. I calculate by my application of Newtons procession, the planet will be at a point where maximum disposition will be made upon the spirit.

Experiment XVI

The whole being finally assembled, I set about preparing for the experiment based upon my previous findings and methodologies.

The remarkable stature of the lifeless body now sewn together, its skin stretched, taught as a tanned hide over grafted muscles, appears as a god of the ages.

After raising the head clear of the bath, I attach the tube to the entry to the skull. It is ready to receive the quantity of elixir as prepared and the galvanic instruments are attached to their points. A continuous supply of Lavoisier's dephlogisticated air will carry over the face of the subject for the duration of this final experiment.

I hesitate and consider it is possible that I have acted in a haste which will have a degrading affect upon the success of my work, only time will speak of whether my impetuousness is considered to be rash or one of genius.

November 29th

By continuous experiment and trial, I have discovered the components and the precise mix of such necessary to re-engage the spirit… I have revitalized tissues now it is time to bestow animation upon my creation.

So, it was on this dreary night, after 1 a.m. that I beheld the accomplishment of my toils. I observed the dull yellow eye of the creature open; it breathed hard, and a convulsive motion agitated its limbs independent of any galvanic activity.

Thus, the compounds of life distilled. I found the recipe which engages the spirit, once released to the ether, to return to inert flesh without resistance. The bridge between death and life connecting the elements. Compounds mixed and then circulated to be in contact with the biological fabric of human tissue revitalizes its energy. The fluid, a precise reconstruction with a certain ratio, manifests a mechanism where energy becomes unrestricted, imbuing expired matter to live again.

The brain energized, the spirit returned to the body. They are as one, they are attached. I have achieved that which I set myself, to renew life to a body where death had placed its icy fingers. My task is complete, I have created life!

But is it the life I anticipated it would be? The yellow skin barely covering the mass of muscles and arteries beneath; the pale, shriveled complexion and straight black lips gave rise to an ugliness even I have not set eyes on before.

Exhausted by the wonder, yet horror of my success, I withdraw this night to my bed and shall report more fully on the outcome when I am recovered, tomorrow.

(Editor's note: The journal ends here - No additional entries)

EPILOGUE – FRANKENSTEIN 2035

1

WAITING

16:35 hrs. October 13th, 2035. Terror Bay, King William Island, Nunavut. Temperature 0° C.

Surrounded by darkness, the spirit hung without constraint, outside of time. There was no wait, there was no time.

The flesh of the vessel which once carried it hollow, indifferent to the life it once supported.

Seeking a release from its pain those years ago, the spirit had urged its physical embodiment to accept the fate it was due. Lungs purging their air as the body jerked its last breath. Without escape the form had flailed, its gaping mouth gulping the suffocating waters, struggling to welcome them to fill the volume of its airways to the brim. Icy cold sea water percolating through hundreds of tiny alveoli, expelling any remnant of physical presence. Fingers clawed at walls, ceiling and door, the confinement held firm.

In the darkness, the form had remained empty, paused. Frozen in place by its own choice. Stilled for a duration not less than nine times its age, each day noted as they gathered in number. Time measured by the turning of the Earth and the momentary passing of diffuse light as events crept slowly towards an arranged destiny.

Now movement stirred the inert body. The sky playing brightly above its place of rest became energized. Stagnant, the cold, dark waters swirled and stirred around the limp form like a heavy, well-worn overcoat. Not with current or action of tide, but a rhythm synchronized with the invisible energy of the universe which weaved its turmoil blindly overhead.

Invisible a magnetism swelled in the atmosphere. Every cell, every muscle, nerve, and sinew became aware, remaining dormant but ready to react. To accept a new owner.

Silently, an elongated oval silhouette cast its shadow over the body's place of captivity as it cut through the divide between water and air seventy feet above. Shimmering like a desert mirage against the sherbet rainbow beyond, its outline, filled with darkness, engulfed the last remnants of light which flittered around its edge like dying embers of an open fire. It knew forces within the object brought with them salvation.

The body, born once, now welcomed a re-birth. Untethered, the orphaned spirit twisting within the multi-dimensional colored aurora as it waited, longing for a return to its home.

It was ready. Again.